DINOSAURS

TOP THAT! Kids™

Copyright © 2003 Top That! Publishing plc
Top That! USA, 27023 McBean Parkway, #408 Valencia, CA 91355
Top That! USA is a Registered Trademark of Top That! Publishing plc
www.topthatpublishing.com

❶ Contents

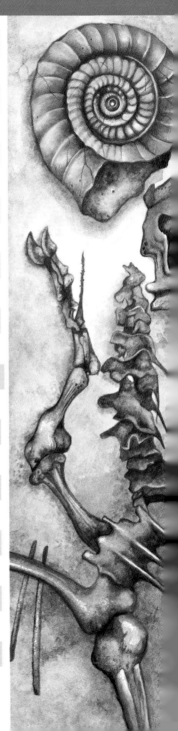

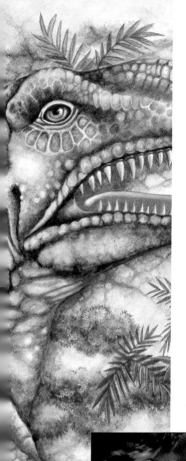

Dinosaurs were a group of animals that lived on Earth until about 65 million years ago.

Scary Monsters

Many of the best-known dinosaurs were enormous, fearsome hunters with huge, sharp teeth and claws. Some were very large, while others were tiny.

Reptiles

Dinosaurs were reptiles. Like the reptiles alive today, they laid eggs and had scaly skin, but unlike their modern relatives, they had long legs underneath their bodies.

Terrible Lizards

It is only since Victorian times that we have begun to properly understand dinosaurs. It was a British scientist, Professor Richard Owen, who discovered that dinosaurs were a group of many different animals, in 1841. He named them dinosaurs— "terrible lizards," and his discovery changed the way people think about life on Earth.

Many Breeds

Many other types of (now extinct) reptiles lived at the same time as the dinosaurs.

Fascinating

We are still fascinated today by these incredible and often terrifying creatures.

Dinosaurs lived on Earth for about 185 million years—about 90 times longer than humans have been around. The time period in which they lived is called the Mesozoic Era.

The Mesozoic Era is divided into three periods—the Triassic, Jurassic and Cretaceous.

Coelophysis lived in the Triassic period.

The Jurassic world, 206-144 million years ago.

Triassic Period
250-206 million years ago

This is the time when the dinosaurs first appeared—small, two-legged meat-eaters and larger plant-eaters. All the land on Earth was joined together in one huge continent that we call Pangaea. The weather was dry and warm, and leafy trees and plants flourished. Other animals included insects, crocodiles and small mammals.

Jurassic Period
206-144 million years ago

This was the time of some of the greatest-ever dinosaurs—mainly huge plant-eaters.

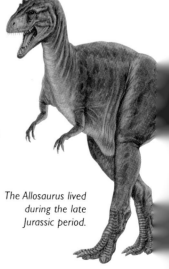

The Allosaurus lived during the late Jurassic period.

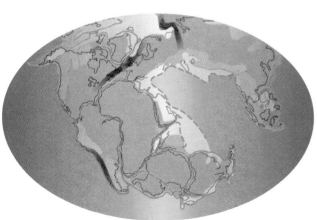

The Triassic world, 250-206 million years ago.

Cretaceous Period
144-65 million years ago

The land had almost split into how it is today. The weather continued to get colder, dividing into wet and dry seasons. The first flowering plants appeared and many large predatory (hunting) dinosaurs lived at this time. By the end of this period, the dinosaurs had died out.

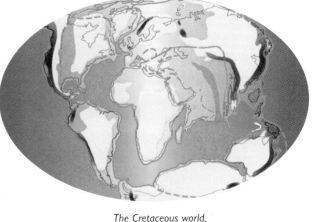

The Cretaceous world, 144-65 million years ago.

Pangaea was beginning to split into separate continents divided by oceans. The weather became cooler and wetter and huge forests began to appear. The first birds appeared and the sky was full of huge, flying reptiles called pterosaurs.

The Tyrannosaurus rex lived during the late Cretaceous period.

After dinosaurs died, they gradually became buried under many layers of sand or mud, which eventually became rock. Dinosaur bones and teeth were preserved in the rock as fossils. Looking at fossils today is how we find out about dinosaurs and other prehistoric creatures.

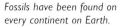

Fossils have been found on every continent on Earth.

Delicate Diggers

Scientists who study dinosaur fossils are called palaeontologists. Sometimes they work in teams to search an area where they think they will find fossils. Many fossils are discovered by accident and these are sent to a palaeontologist to be studied. Detailed records are made of the site, and the fossil is handled very carefully.

A palaeontologist identifying a fossil.

Them Bones

Dinosaur bones can tell us a lot. It's easy to get an idea of what a dinosaur looked like and how big it was from a complete skeleton. Claws and armor will show how it attacked and defended itself and the skull will provide clues as to what it ate.

We can learn a lot from a dinosaur's teeth.

Dinner Time!

Dinosaur teeth can tell us about their diet.

Meat-eaters generally had long, sharp teeth for tearing flesh; plant-eaters' teeth tended to be wider and flatter.

Scaly Skin

Although the skin of dinosaurs has not survived, some fossils have been found with the patterns and texture of the skin imprinted on the rock.

The head and neck structure of a typical theropod.

Changing Color

We can only guess at the color of dinosaurs, which may have depended on the need for camouflage. Some may have been able to change color to warn off others or attract a mate.

7

It is difficult to discover much about dinosaur behaviour and lifestyle from their remains, but many fossil sites contain the remains of large numbers of dinosaurs.

A scavenging Tyrannosaurus rex.

Plant-eating Herds
As they were found together, this suggests that they lived in herds or packs. Plant-eaters probably lived in herds for safety reasons.

Pack Hunters
A large pack of carnivores (meat-eaters) would be able to hunt more effectively than individuals.

Lone Hunters
Tyrannosaurus rex was probably a lone hunter, ambushing its prey with its mouth wide open.

A pack of Coelophysis hunting their prey.

Egg Layers

Most dinosaurs, like reptiles today, laid eggs. Large numbers of fossilized eggs have been found together, meaning that some dinosaurs may have nested together in large groups, or colonies. There is some evidence to suggest that, like birds, they may have returned to the same place to nest year after year.

A nest of baby dinosaurs.

Big Brood

Dinosaurs would have had many babies, but it is thought that very few of them would have been caring parents. One possible exception is the group of dinosaurs known as hadrosaurs. There is evidence to suggest that their young looked very cute—they had big eyes and rounded heads—so their parents may have been more likely to look after them.

A baby hadrosaur.

A hadrosaur tending to her young.

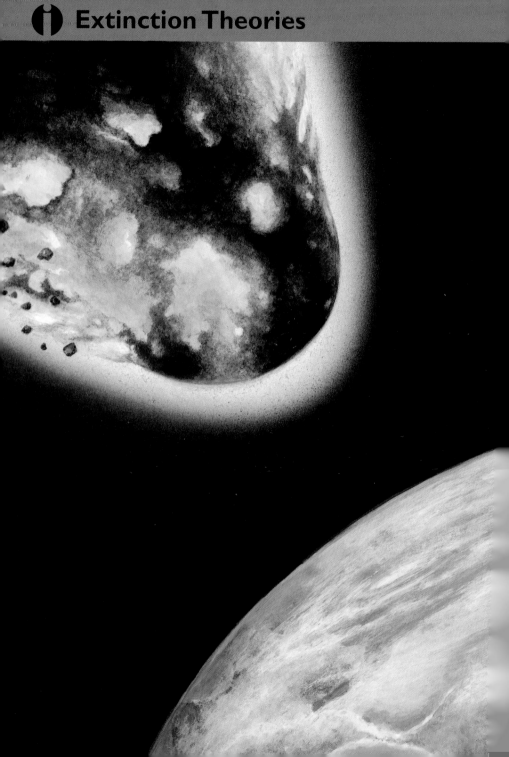

Dinosaurs were one of the most successful groups of animals that ever lived on the Earth. Then, about 65 million years ago, something happened that wiped them out.

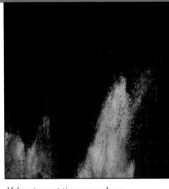

Volcanic eruptions may have killed off the dinosaurs.

Theories

There are many theories about what exactly happened, but most experts agree that it was very sudden and that it affected the whole planet—its climate, plants and animals other than the dinosaurs.

Meteorite

A popular theory is that Earth was hit by a huge meteorite or asteroid from outer space. The impact would have caused a huge explosion, sending up enormous clouds of dust into the atmosphere. This would have blocked out the Sun, creating a long, worldwide winter. Without light and heat, millions of plants and animals would have died out, including the dinosaurs.

Large clouds of dust could have blocked out light and heat.

Volcanic Eruptions

Other experts suggest that volcanic eruptions may have been responsible. These could have burnt up the oxygen in the atmosphere, making it difficult for living things to breathe.

Deadly Disease

Some experts think that dinosaur extinction was a slower process. Some kind of deadly disease could have killed them, or changing vegetation may have poisoned them to death. Also, the new types of mammals that were appearing may have eaten the dinosaur eggs.

Putting dinosaurs into different groups is not easy. There are many different types and the relationships between them are not always clear. Plus, new research about dinosaurs often changes their names or places them in different groups.

Ornithischians had pubis bones that pointed downward and to the front, like those of birds.

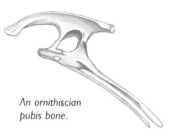

An ornithiscian pubis bone.

Division
Dinosaurs are normally divided into two main orders (groups) which classify them according to the shape of their hip bones. The groups are called saurischia ("lizard-hipped") and ornithischia ("bird-hipped").

In a saurischian skeleton, the pubis bone of the hip points down and to the back, like that of a lizard.

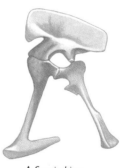

A Saurischian pubis bone.

Meat and Vegetables
Saurischians are divided into two groups: the fast, meat-eating theropods and the large, plant-eating sauropods. The sauropods appeared first but the theropods remained until the end of the dinosaur age.

Tyrannosaurus rex was a theropod—a saurischian dinosaur.

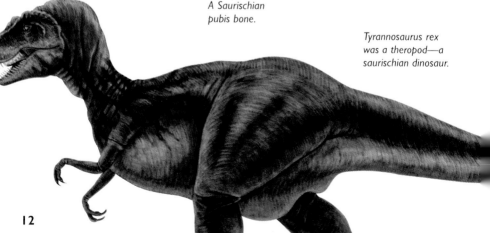

Ornithischian Family

There are five groups of ornithischians: ankylosaurs, ceratopsians, ornithopods, pachycephalosaurs and stegosaurs. All of the dinosaurs in these groups were plant-eaters and some developed armor plating, horns or spikes to defend themselves against predators.

Triceratops was a ceratopsian—an ornithischian dinosaur.

Iguanodon was an ornithopod—an ornithischian dinosaur.

The Bird Question

Interestingly, birds are believed to have evolved from the saurischians, rather than the ornithischians (see page 35).

Euoplocephalus was an ankylosaur—an ornithischian dinosaur.

13

The theropod group of saurischian dinosaurs contained some of the most fearsome carnivorous (meat-eating) creatures ever to walk the Earth, including Allosaurus (pages 30-31) and Tyrannosaurus rex (pages 32-33).

Large Hunters

These large hunters all walked (and ran) on their rear legs—the front legs were often tiny. Their heads were large and their mouths were filled with many razor-sharp teeth. Their long tails helped them to balance.

Fearsome Find

One of the first theropods to be identified and named was Megalosaurus, which means "big reptile." Remains were found in Oxfordshire, England in 1824.

Hunters and Scavengers

While the largest of the theropods probably hunted and scavenged for food alone, some of the smaller ones are thought to have hunted in packs. Deinonychus was one such creature. Its name means "terrible claw," which describes the lethal curved claws that it had on the second toe of each foot. A group of Deinonychus' would leap on their prey and slash at it.

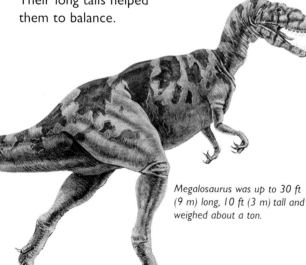

Megalosaurus was up to 30 ft (9 m) long, 10 ft (3 m) tall and weighed about a ton.

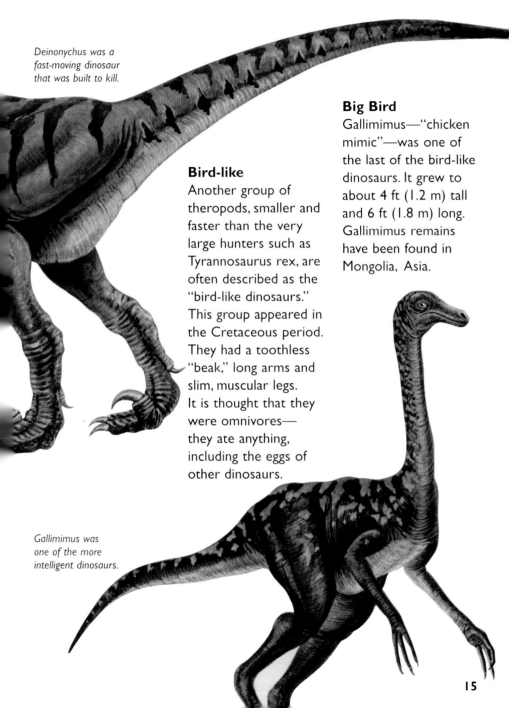

Deinonychus was a fast-moving dinosaur that was built to kill.

Bird-like

Another group of theropods, smaller and faster than the very large hunters such as Tyrannosaurus rex, are often described as the "bird-like dinosaurs." This group appeared in the Cretaceous period. They had a toothless "beak," long arms and slim, muscular legs. It is thought that they were omnivores—they ate anything, including the eggs of other dinosaurs.

Big Bird

Gallimimus—"chicken mimic"—was one of the last of the bird-like dinosaurs. It grew to about 4 ft (1.2 m) tall and 6 ft (1.8 m) long. Gallimimus remains have been found in Mongolia, Asia.

Gallimimus was one of the more intelligent dinosaurs.

15

Sauropods

The sauropods included some of the largest creatures ever to walk the Earth. Appearing during the Jurassic period, these enormous vegetarians had long necks and tails and bulky bodies. They walked on all four legs, but could rear up on to their back legs to reach the leaves of tall trees. As the sauropods evolved, they got bigger and bigger. The biggest of all was Brachiosaurus (pages 40-41).

Brachiosaurus was the tallest of the sauropods.

Stretch and Reach
Diplodocus is one of the best-known of this type of dinosaur. It was quite slim for a sauropod, but was one of the longest, measuring up to 89 ft (27 m) mainly due to its long neck and tail.

Down in One

Sauropods' teeth were a bit like clothes pins—long and flat and no use for chewing. They closed their mouth around the leaves of trees, and stripped them off, swallowing them whole.

Astrodon (meaning "star-tooth") was a long-necked, plant-eating sauropod that is known only from fossilized teeth found in Maryland, USA.

Diplodocus' long neck was probably used to get to food that other sauropods couldn't reach.

Quick-footed

No one is really sure why the sauropods grew to be so large, but such huge creatures were less likely to suffer attacks from smaller predators. Despite their size, it is thought that sauropods could move quite quickly. Their foot bones were similar to those of modern elephants— large animals able to move at speed. However, it is unlikely that they were able to run.

Balancing Act

A sauropod's skeleton was immensely strong. The weight of the long neck and tail was balanced over the back legs.

17

The ornithischian ankylosaurs were small to medium-sized dinosaurs. The main feature of these plant-eaters, which lived during the Cretaceous period, was their armor of bony plates or spikes.

These would have been especially useful when the dinosaur was being attacked by a large, vicious predator.

Armored Tanks
Ankylosaurs had broad, low bodies and were covered in bony, patterned plates. Their heads were small and heavily armored. It is thought that ankylosaurs had a good sense of smell.

Several of the ankylosaurs, including Polacanthus and Ankylosaurus (see pages 44-45), had spikes.

Safety First
It is thought that Polacanthus would crouch low to the ground, using its spiked armor to protect itself.

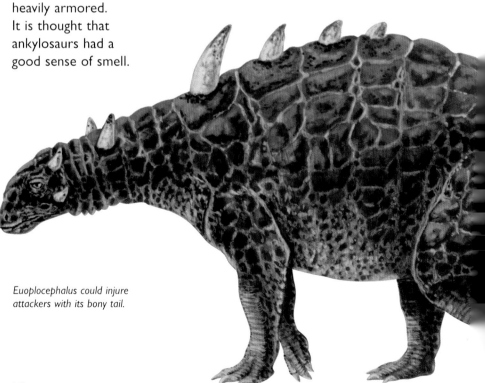

Euoplocephalus could injure attackers with its bony tail.

Polacanthus crouched low to protect itself from predators.

This is similar to the way that a hedgehog might protect itself today.

A hedgehog's spikes work like an ankylosaur's spikes.

Swing That Tail!

Some ankylosaurs, including the Euoplocephalus and Ankylosaurus, had a bony club at the end of their tail. A powerful swing of the tail could easily topple, or even injure, a large theropod attacker.

The clubs may have measured up to 1 m (3 ft) across. The muscles of an ankylosaur's tail would have been extremely powerful.

Sink or Swim

It is thought that ankylosaurs tended to avoid areas where there were lots of rivers and lakes, as their heavy armor would have made swimming almost impossible.

The ceratopsians were a group of plant-eaters that appeared during the Cretaceous period. They had a sharp, beak-like mouth, much like a parrot's. Their teeth were good for chewing, as were their powerful jaws.

Triceratops.

Efficient Eating
The ceratopsians were able to eat the toughest of plants, such as the flowering magnolia plants that began to appear in the Cretaceous period.

Globe Trotters
Many remains of Protoceratops have been found in Mongolia. These range from complete nests of eggs, to the bones of adults.

Effective Armor
The most distinctive features of most of the ceratopsians were the horns on their heads and the bony plate above their necks. These would have been useful for defending themselves from an attack by predators, but many dinosaur experts think that they were mainly used for fighting each other. It's easy to imagine a pair of rival male Centrosaurus' or Triceratops' (see pages 46-47) locked in battle like deer today.

Centrosaurus had a large single nose horn, like a rhinoceros.

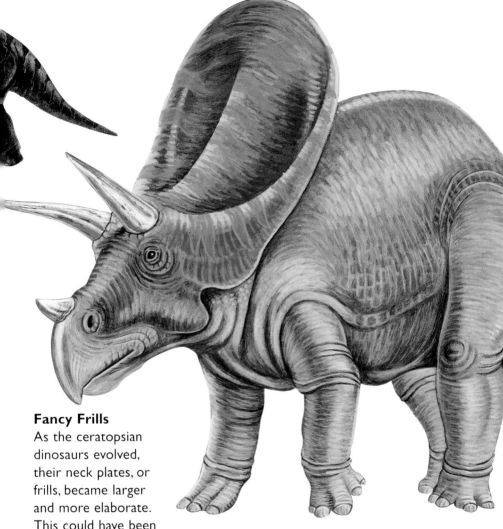

Fancy Frills

As the ceratopsian dinosaurs evolved, their neck plates, or frills, became larger and more elaborate. This could have been for "social" reasons. Ceratopsians were most likely to be herd animals and a large, fancy-looking frill might have shown who was the leader of a group.

Showing Off

Torosaurus had the largest frill of any of the ceratopsians— longer even than its own skull, which in itself was up to 8.5 ft (2.6 m) long!

Torosaurus had a reduced nose horn and well-developed eyebrow horns.

21

The group of dinosaurs known as the ornithopods includes one of the first dinosaurs to be studied, Iguanodon (see pages 38-39), and a further family of dinosaurs called hadrosaurs.

Hadrosaurs were the only dinosaurs whose teeth were continually replaced by new ones.

Clever Chewers

The ornithopods appeared in the late Jurassic period, about 150 million years ago. They were probably the first of the plant-eaters that were able to chew their food well. Ornithopods also had fleshy cheek pockets to prevent their food falling out while they were chewing.

Puffed Up

The hadrosaurs are known for their duck-like beaks and various strangely shaped skulls. Edmontosaurus' had loose flaps of skin which they could inflate, probably to communicate and show off.

Getting Attention

Parasaurolophus was the hadrosaur with the most extremely developed head. The long, curved crest on the top of its skull was hollow and connected to its nose. These were much larger in males and it is thought that they were used to create a long, hooting sound. The bigger the crest the louder the hoot!

Safety in Numbers

None of the ornithopods appear to have had many ways of defending themselves, but they do seem to have lived together in large groups, which may have given some protection and suggests they were social creatures.

Swift Swimmers

The hadrosaurs had quite wide, paddle-shaped hands, which could have been used for swimming. This trait would have provided a useful method of escape.

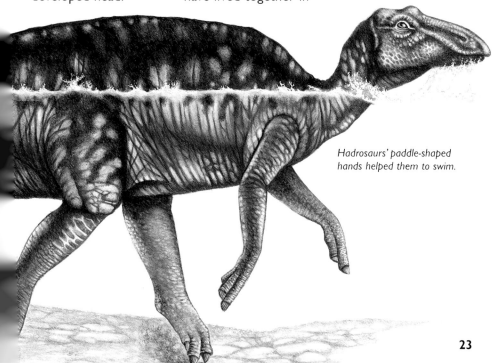

Hadrosaurs' paddle-shaped hands helped them to swim.

23

Known as the "head-banging" dinosaurs, the pachycephalosaurs appeared toward the end of the dinosaur age, in the late Cretaceous period. Their skulls had a thick dome on the top, which was up to 10 in. (25 cm) thick.

The skull of a pachycephalosaur.

Little Guys
The majority of the group were relatively small—Stegoceras being only 8 ft (2.4 m) long. However, Pachycephalosaurus was an impressive 15 ft (4.6 m) in length.

Shock Tactics
The extremely thick skulls of the pachycephalosaurs were probably used to ram attackers, or as many experts believe, in displays of strength.

Head-butting competitions would take place, in order to impress the females in their group.

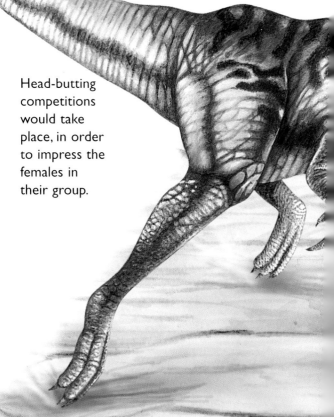

Good Support

The very heavy skull was connected to the rest of the body in a way that would have supported it well and absorbed the shock of head-butting. Its neck bones were very thick.

Scant Remains

Skeletons and other remains of pachycephalosaurs are rarely found—an entire skeleton is yet to be discovered. Most of the remains have been found in North America. Most experts think that the lack of fossilized remains means that they probably lived in very dry areas—places where remains would not be very well preserved.

Boneheads

The skull of a pachycephalosaur makes it look like a large-brained, intelligent creature. Unfortunately, with so much of it being made of bone, these dinosaurs are known as the "boneheads"!

A pair of pachycephalosaurs fighting.

Stegosaurs

The stegosaurs are named after the best-known member of the group—Stegosaurus (pages 42-43). They are identified by the rows of bony plates along the length of their back.

It was once thought that the plates lay flat on the stegosaur's back like the tiles on a roof—"stegosaur" means "roof lizard."

Holey Plates
It is unlikely that the plates would have protected stegosaurs from an attack as they are not solid but have honeycomb-like cavities (spaces) inside.

Solar Panels
Scientists believe that they would have been used to help the stegosaur control its body temperature. They would have helped it funnel a breeze over its body to cool down, and to collect heat from the Sun when it was too cold.

Easy Target
Stegosaurs were large, slow-moving creatures that fed on vegetation, mostly on the ground. It is thought that they would have been an easy target for predators. Their only

form of defense was their heavily-spiked tail, which they would swing using the powerful muscles in their tails.

The skeleton of a stegosaur.

Asian Discovery

Several complete stegosaur skeletons have been found in China. Tuojiangosaurus is one of the best-known

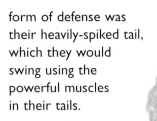

examples and was the first stegosaur ever to be discovered in Asia. It had all the classic features of a stegosaur. Most of the weight of the animal was supported on its rear legs.

Stegosaurus weighed about 6,800 pounds (3,100 kg).

Coelophysis is one of the earliest-known dinosaurs, living around 220 million years ago. It was small, lightly-built and walked on its rear legs. It was probably very fast. Its hollow bones and long legs made it very light and quite athletic.

Not Fussy!
As a carnivore, its speed would have been very useful. Like many meat-eaters, Coelophysis was probably a scavenger as well. Fossilized remains of small reptiles and fish have been found inside

The Coelophysis would have been approximately two-thirds as tall as a man.

them. There is also some evidence that they would they would have eaten each other!

Snake-like Neck
Coelophysis had a very long, narrow head and jaws at the end of a long neck. It had lots of very sharp, serrated (saw-like) teeth. Its arms had useful, grasping hands with fingers strong enough to grasp prey.

Desert Living
Edwin Colbert's discovery of the first complete Coelophysis skeleton in 1947 was followed by the discovery of many more remains at Ghost Ranch, New Mexico, USA, which turned out to be a massive bone bed, containing several complete skeletons.

Group:	Saurischia, theropod
Height:	4 ft (1.2 m)
Length:	10 ft (3 m)
When it lived:	Triassic period, 210 million years ago
Fossils found in:	North America

Space Dinosaur
A Coelophysis skull from the Carnegie Museum of Natural History was taken into space by the space shuttle *Endeavour* in 1998. It spent time on the space station *Mir*.

Coelophysis means "hollow form." This dinosaur had light, hollow bones.

The complete fossilized remains of a Coelophysis.

Allosaurus was a large, powerful meat-eater with a massive tail. Its vertebrae (back bones) were different from other similar dinosaurs, a fact that gives Allosaurus its name—"different reptile."

Allosaurus had large, powerful jaws with long, sharp teeth up to 2-4 in. (5-10 cm) long.

"Top Dog"

Its arms were short, but were quite strong with long claws. Like other large theropods, it had big, powerful jaws with very sharp teeth. Its skull was about 3 ft (90 cm) long and it had bony brows and ridges above its eyes. It probably hunted and ate small to medium-sized sauropods and was the top predator in the Jurassic period. They were not rivaled in size until the tyrannosaurs appeared in the Cretaceous period.

Lie in Wait

The big question about Allosaurus and other large meat-eaters is whether they could have run very fast. Many scientists believe that if the Allosaurus fell over at speed, it would injure itself very badly. It is therefore more likely that Allosaurus would hide and wait for its prey to get near and then pounce. Slower, injured animals would have been its most likely targets.

Happy Eater
Whichever way Allosaurus caught its food, seeing it eat would have been a terrifying sight. Its powerful jaw and neck muscles allowed it to tear huge lumps of flesh from its victim and swallow them whole. After a big meal, Allosaurus would have laid down on the ground and basked in the Sun.

Group:	Saurischia, theropod
Height:	16.5 ft (5 m)
Length:	39 ft (12 m)
When it lived:	Late Jurassic period, 150 million years ago
Fossils found in:	North America, Australia

Tyrannosaurus rex—"the lizard king," is probably the best-known of all the dinosaurs, as it is always featured in movies and stories about prehistoric creatures, such as *The Land That Time Forgot* and *Jurassic Park*.

It is famous as the biggest predator ever to have lived on land, although others have since been discovered (Giganotosaurus, pages 36-37) that are bigger.

Replacement Teeth

Despite losing its crown as the biggest meat-eater, T. rex was still one of the fiercest predators. Its huge mouth was filled with very strong, pointed teeth that were up to 9 in. (23 cm) long. Its teeth were replaced as they wore down or broke off.

Greedy Guts

They were capable of crunching bone and scientists think that they were able to swallow as much as 500 pounds (230 kg) of meat and bone at once!

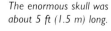

T. rex had a stride length up to 15 ft (4.6 m).

The enormous skull was about 5 ft (1.5 m) long.

Heavy Mover?

As with the other large theropods, there is some mystery about the speed a T. rex could run. Some scientists think that it could have run at up to 15 mph (24 kph). T. rex's tail may have helped to control it at speed, as it was slim and stiff and helped the dinosaur to balance.

Tiny Arms

For such a fearsome beast, the T. rex had tiny little arms and claws, which were not much use. It is thought that T. rex may therefore have had a problem getting up if it fell over.

Group:	Saurischia, theropod
Height:	20 ft (6 m)
Length:	46 ft (14 m)
When it lived:	Late Cretaceous period, 70 million years ago
Fossils found in:	North America

Compsognathus

Compsognathus was the smallest of all known dinosaurs, weighing only 8 lb (3-6 kg). Most of the skeletons found are about the size of a large chicken, though both larger and smaller examples exist.

Dino Digits
Its arms were short and it had two clawed fingers on each hand. Each foot included a tiny toe pointing backwards.

Run For It
Compsognathus was one of the bird-like theropods and, being so small and with hollow bones, it would have been a very fast runner. It ate meat, chewing up insects and small lizards with its tiny, sharp teeth. It would have been a good scavenger—easily able to find scraps and able to escape larger predators and outrun other scavengers.

Forest Forage
Compsognathus probably lived in dense, forested areas where there was plenty of food and where it could hide from larger creatures.

Bird Mystery

Compsognathus is an important part of one of the great dinosaur mysteries—did birds evolve from them? The skeleton of Compsognathus is very similar to that of a feathered, bird-like creature, Archaeopteryx.

Archaeopteryx lived at about the same time as Compsognathus and had feathered wings with claws at the end. Scientists are still trying to work out if it was a bird (it probably could not fly) or simply a dinosaur with wings.

Bird or dinosaur?

Compsognathus was a bird-like dinosaur designed for speed.

Group:	Saurischia, theropod
Height:	Up to 2 ft (60 cm)
Length:	Up to 4.6 ft (1.4 m)
When it lived:	Late Jurassic period, 150 million years ago
Fossils found in:	Germany, France

Giganotosaurus was the biggest meat-eater ever to walk the Earth. It lived about 30 million years before its close relative, Tyrannosaurus rex.

Fearsome Hunter
The teeth of Gigantosaurus were about 8 in. (20 cm) long. They were sharp and knife-like.

Banana Brain
Weighing in at about eight tons, Giganotosaurus was literally gigantic. Although it was bigger than T. rex, it was more lightly built and could have been able to move more quickly. It also had a much smaller brain than T. rex, about the size and shape of a banana.

Gigantosaurus weighed about 8 tons.

Group:	Saurischia, theropod
Height:	Up to 25 ft (7.6 m)
Length:	Up to 50 ft (15 m)
When it lived:	Cretaceous period, 100 million years ago
Fossils found in:	South America

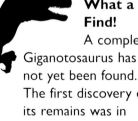

What a Find!

A complete Giganotosaurus has not yet been found. The first discovery of its remains was in Argentina in 1994. Its name means "giant southern lizard." It was discovered not by an expert palaeontologist, but by a car mechanic whose hobby was looking for dinosaur fossils. His name was Ruben Carolini and this huge dinosaur has been given the scientific name Giganotosaurus carolinii in his honor.

The fossils of the Iguanodon were among the first to be discovered. They were found in England in 1809—before the word "dinosaur" had been invented. Their discoverer, Gideon Mantell, realized that the teeth were similar to those of the iguana—a modern lizard.

Large Brain

For a dinosaur, it had quite a large brain and good senses. It is thought that they may have lived in social groups and cared well for their young.

Human Habits

Iguanodon was a fairly large, plant-eating dinosaur. At the front of its mouth was a horned, toothless beak which it used to nip at vegetation. At the back, in its cheeks, were many rows of teeth. These were excellent for chewing a wide range of plants. It is thought that Iguanodon chewed and swallowed its food in much the same way as people do.

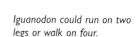

Iguanodon could run on two legs or walk on four.

Iguanodon's teeth were at the back of the mouth.

Iguanodon

Group:	Saurischia, theropod
Height:	16 ft (5 m)
Length:	30 ft (9.3 m)
When it lived:	Early Cretaceous period, 130 million years ago
Fossils found in:	Britain, North Africa, Asia

Fingers and Thumbs

Iguanodon's arms were long and strong. They had hands with four fingers and a thumb. They would have walked either on two legs or on all fours. The thumb was equipped with a large spike, which was used for defense and finding food. It might also have been used to fight rivals in the same social group.

Brachiosaurus

Brachiosaurus was the tallest and largest of all the massive, plant-eating sauropods. Walking on all four legs, it used its very long neck and long front legs to reach the leaves at the tops of trees, and had a posture very similar to the giraffe.

Heavyweights

These huge creatures were among the heaviest of all dinosaurs, weighing up to 88 tons. The legs of the Brachiosaurus had to bear all the weight of the body whilst moving. We refer to such creatures as "graviportal" or "heavy carrying."

Water Wonder

It used to be thought that Brachiosaurus spent most of its time in water, much like hippos today.

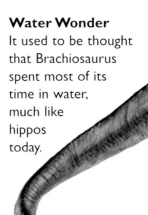

Its nostrils were placed high on its forehead, suggesting that they could have been used a bit like a snorkel. While most scientists now agree that it lived on land, there is some evidence that it would have waded in lakes and rivers. It may have done this to feed on

water plants. It is thought that healthy adult Brachiosaurus' were safe from predators. They were twice the size of the

meat-eating theropods that lived at the time and there was plenty of easier prey around.

The legs of the Brachiosaurus had to bear all the weight while moving.

Stone Swallowers

A great many Brachiosaurus' (and other sauropods) skeletons have been found with small stones in their stomachs. It is thought that these were swallowed by the young dinosaur to help it mash up and digest food in its stomach.

Group:	Saurischia, sauropod
Height:	39 ft (12 m)
Length:	74 ft (22.5 m)
When it lived:	Jurassic period, 150 million years ago
Fossils found in:	North America, Africa

The largest of all the stegosaurs, Stegosaurus is famous for the plates on its back and also for its small brain—the smallest of all the dinosaurs.

Mate Plate
Stegosaurus had seventeen bony plates on its back and tail. As well as controlling body temperature (see pages 26-27), it's possible that the males used their plates to attract a mate.

Angry Tail
Stegosaurs' spiked tails were used as weapons. The tail had eight of these spikes, each up to 4 ft (1.2 m) long.

Attention!
Some scientists believe the plates would flush pink during courting. This would also happen when a fight was imminent as a threat display. Scientists are unsure whether the plates laid flat or upright.

Stegosaurus' back legs were twice as long as its front legs.

Group:	Ornithischia, stegosaur
Height:	Up to 15.7 ft (4.7 m)
Length:	Up to 30 ft (9 m)
When it lived:	Jurassic period, 150 million years ago
Fossils found in:	North America

Walnut Brain

Stegosaurus is famous for having a very small brain—often described as being the "size of a walnut." Scientists compare the size of a dinosaur's brain with the rest of its body to guess its intelligence. As Stegosaurus was very large (as big as a large truck), it was probably not very clever.

Predators

This herbivore would have been preyed on by the fierce carnivore Allosaurus (pages 30-31).

Weighing around 4.4 tons, Ankylosaurus was the largest member of the ankylosaur family, the "fused together lizards." It lived at the end of the age of the dinosaurs.

It lived at the same time as the fearsome Tyrannosaurus rex (see pages 32-33), a dinosaur that was probably one of its predators.

Heavy Duty
Ankylosaurus was heavily protected by its bony plates and spikes. Even its eyes were protected.

Soft Underbelly
The only way a predator would have been able to attack Ankylosaurus would be to flip it over—its underbelly was unprotected. Most would probably give up and look for easier prey.

The Pink One
As with the plates of a Stegosaurus, the body armor of this dinosaur may also have turned pink after being filled with blood, earning it the nickname the "blushing dinosaur."

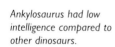

Ankylosaurus had low intelligence compared to other dinosaurs.

Pardon Me!
Ankylosaurus' diet was limited to the plants that it found close to the ground. Some scientists think that this meant its stomach would have produced an enormous amount of gas!

Group:	Ornithischia, ankylosaur
Height:	10 ft (3 m)
Length:	33 ft (10 m)
When it lived:	Late Cretaceous period, 70 million years ago
Fossils found in:	North and South America

Triceratops—"three-horned face"—is one of the best-known dinosaurs. Living at the end of the dinosaur age, it was the largest of the ceratopsians. It is often compared to the rhinoceros of today. An adult Triceratops however, would be around twice the size of a rhino.

Fighting

It is thought that the horns were used to fight rivals, but they would have been an excellent way of attacking a predator. It would have charged at its attacker (T. rex lived at the same time), in much the same way as a rhino does.

Bony

The bony horns and neck plate are the most distinctive features of Triceratops and most of the other ceratopsians. It had one short horn above its parrot-like beak and two longer horns, just above its eyes.

Triceratops had a large skull, up to 10 ft (3 m) long.

Group:	Ornithischia, ceratopsian
Height:	13 ft (4 m)
Length:	30 ft (9 m)
When it lived:	Late Cretaceous period, 70 million years ago
Fossils found in:	North America

Bit Common

Triceratops was a very common dinosaur and many fossil examples have been found, mostly in western North America. When the fossils were first discovered in the late nineteenth century, they were thought to belong to an extinct species of buffalo.

Research into dinosaurs is going on all the time. Fossils are found, palaeontologists discuss theories about them, and new ways of studying dinosaurs are developed.

Museums

Museums all over the world have displays of some of the best dinosaur remains. Many of them have complete skeletons and life-size models of dinosaurs. This is the best way to see what these incredible creatures were like for yourself.

On Screen

Dinosaurs continue to be the subject of science fiction films. Some of them have suggested that dinosaur remains could be used to bring them back to life. Scientists all agree that this is impossible… for now!

Acknowledgments
Key: Top - t; middle - m; bottom - b; left - l; right - r. Science Photo Library - SPL.
Front cover: (m) John Butler; (ml,mr) Corel. Back cover: Corel. **1:** Top That! **2:** John Butler. **3:** (ml) Corel, (m) Top That!; (r) Peter Menzel/SPL.
4: (tl,br) Corel; (tr,bl) TTAT. **5:** (t) TTAT; (b) Corel. **6:** (t,br) Top That!; (bl) Corel. **7:** (t,bl) Top That!, (mr) James Field. **8:** (t) Corel; (b) John Butler.
9: (t) Top That! (m,b)John Butler. **10:** John Butler. **11:** (t) Corel; (b) John Butler. **12:** (t,m) TTAT; (b) Corel. **13:** Corel. **14/15:** Corel. **16/17:** Corel.
18: Corel. **19:** (t) John Butler; (m) Top That!. **20:** (t,b) Corel. **21:** John Butler. **22:** Corel. **23:** John Butler. **24/25:** John Butler.
27: (t) James Field; (b) Corel. **28:** (b) TTAT. **29:** (ml) Corel; (mr) Sinclair Stammers/SPL. **31:** (l) Corel; (r) TTAT. **32:** (b) Top That!.
33: (l) Corel; (m) TTAT. **34:** (t) Corel; (b) TTAT. **35:** Corel. **36:** John Butler. **37:** (b) TTAT. **38:** (m) Corel; (b) John Butler. **39:** (b) TTAT. **40:** Corel.
41: (m) TTAT. **42:** Corel. **43:** (m) TTAT. **45:** (m) Corel; (br) TTAT. **46:** (bl) TTAT; (r) Corel. **48:** (t) James Field. (b) Peter Menzel/SPL.